LOVE ACROSS THE MERIDIAN

SWATI SINGH

BlueRoseONE.com
Stories Matter
NewDelhi • London

BLUEROSE PUBLISHERS
India | U.K.

For permissions requests or inquiries regarding this publication, please contact:

BLUEROSE PUBLISHERS
www.BlueRoseONE.com
info@bluerosepublishers.com
+91 8882 898 898
+4407342408967

ISBN: 978-93-7542-441-3

Cover Design: Shivam Gaur
Typesetting: Sagar

First Edition: March 2026

Prologue

She was chasing stories around the world.

He was listening to the ocean, waiting for one to find him.

When Maya Kapoor, a travel filmmaker from Mumbai, lands in Lisbon for a documentary, she's only supposed to capture love – not fall into it.

But when she meets Elias Rocha, a marine biologist with the calm of the sea in his voice, something in her shifts.

What begins as a fleeting encounter turns into late-night calls, letters carried by tides, and promises whispered across time zones.

Yet distance has a way of testing what the heart builds.

As the world spins between them – between airports, oceans, and the silence of missed messages – Maya and Elias must decide if love can survive when it's stretched across the meridian.

A story of longing, courage, and the beautiful ache of finding home in someone halfway across the world,

Love Across the Meridian is a romance for anyone who has ever loved beyond borders – and believed that some hearts are destined to meet, no matter how far they drift.

Contents

Chapter 1.

The Flight That Changed Everything

The boarding gate at Chhatrapati Shivaji International Airport buzzed with overlapping announcements and the soft clatter of rolling suitcases.

Maya Kapoor adjusted her backpack strap, eyes fixed on her phone screen – one unread message from her ex, still sitting there like a ghost she refused to open.

"Flight AI-147 to Lisbon is now boarding," echoed over the speakers.

She sighed. "Finally," she muttered, more to herself than anyone else. A month-long project overseas – that was exactly what she needed. New faces, new places, and no chance of running into the past.

As she moved toward the gate, the familiar weight of her camera bag dug into her shoulder – both comfort and burden. The camera had been her constant companion, her silent witness through heartbreaks and triumphs alike. Her new documentary, Love Across the Meridian, aimed to capture real love stories from around the world – ironic, given that she no longer believed in the concept.

Inside the aircraft, the air smelled faintly of coffee and jet fuel. Maya found her seat by the window – 17A. She tucked her camera case beneath the seat in front, plugged in her earphones, and prepared to zone out. But fate, it seemed, had other plans.

"Excuse me," came a voice – warm, deep, faintly accented.

She looked up. A tall man stood in the aisle, trying to fit a large duffel bag into the overhead compartment. His dark curls fell slightly over his forehead, and his shirt sleeves were rolled just enough to reveal tanned, lean forearms. The aisle light caught the glint of a silver bracelet on his wrist.

"I think your backpack strap is caught in the armrest," he said with a polite smile. "If you move it, I can fit this through."

"Oh! Right, sorry," Maya fumbled, freeing the strap. "These seats are not made for human comfort."

He chuckled softly. "Nor for tall people. It's a global conspiracy, I'm sure."

She smiled despite herself – the first genuine one in weeks. As he settled into the seat beside her, she noticed his eyes – sea-grey, calm yet full of stories. Something about him reminded her of unspoken poetry.

"I'm Elias," he said, extending a hand. "Lisbon native. You?"

"Maya. From Mumbai. Filmmaker." She hesitated, then added, "Documentary, not Bollywood."

He grinned. "Ah, disappointment. I was hoping for a cameo in the next big song sequence."

She laughed – a quick, involuntary sound that surprised her. "Trust me, I don't sing or dance on planes."

"Pity," he teased. "Would make the flight more interesting."

The seatbelt sign flickered on. The engines hummed with a rising, steady confidence.

As the plane lifted off the runway, the city lights of Mumbai blurred into a shimmering sea of gold – a thousand glowing stories fading beneath them.

Maya pressed her forehead lightly to the window for a moment, watching the lights drift away like fireflies. When she leaned back, she found Elias watching her with a polite, curious smile – the kind strangers exchanged before deciding whether to speak or stay silent.

She chose to speak.

"Do you ever look down and wonder how many lives are unfolding at this exact moment?" she asked softly.

Elias followed her gaze to the fading city.
"All the time," he said. "Everyone moving with their own tides."

A small laugh escaped her.
"That sounds like something a poet would say."

"Marine biologist," he corrected playfully. "But... I spend enough time with the ocean to start speaking like it."

That made her smile. And it made her ask the next question.

"So what takes you across continents? Work?"

"Mostly." Elias shifted to face her more fully. "Coral reef mapping. Ocean temperature studies. The boring explanation is: I look at data all day. The romantic explanation is: I try to understand how the ocean breathes."

"That's not boring," Maya said, eyes widening. "It's beautiful."

He shrugged, a little shy.
"Beauty depends on who's listening."

They fell into conversation then – the kind that flows effortlessly, like water finding its own path.

She told him about her film.
"Love Across the Meridian," she said. "Stories of people trying to hold on to something despite distance, culture, time zones... reality."

"And you?" he asked. "Have you ever loved across a continent?"

Maya's gaze flickered downward.
"I've loved across expectations. That was hard enough." She paused, then added with a soft smile, "But I believe in the idea. Distance doesn't scare me. A lack of effort does."

Elias nodded slowly, as though absorbing every word.
"That's fair."

Then she returned the question.
"And you? Have you loved across a continent?"

He chuckled, scratching the back of his neck.
"I've loved across oceans, technically. But not romantically." He paused for a moment, choosing his words carefully.

"You spend enough time with the water... you form a relationship with it."

That intrigued her, so she leaned in.
"And the ocean is your great love?"

"The ocean," he said, with surprising softness, "is the most faithful lover there is."

Maya blinked, taken aback by the unexpected poetry in his tone.
"Why?" she asked.

He looked out the window – at the darkening sky, at the invisible horizon – then back at her.

"Because no matter how many storms you face," he said, "it always comes back to kiss the shore."

Her breath caught – not because of the words alone, but because of the way he said them.
Quietly.
Truthfully.
As if he had lived the metaphor, not just spoken it.

"That's..." Maya paused, searching for the right word. "Romantic."

"It's scientific," he insisted, though the corner of his mouth betrayed a smile.
"Nature always returns."

"Maybe people do too," she whispered.

"Some," he said. "Not all."

Their shoulders brushed when the plane dipped slightly. Neither moved away.

The conversation drifted again –
from reefs to film festivals,
from currents to childhood dreams,
from fears they admitted softly to hopes they almost didn't share.

Silences came, but they were warm.
Comfortable.
Like the quiet between two waves preparing to meet.

When the cabin lights dimmed, Maya pulled her blanket a little closer.
Elias adjusted his seat.

And for the first time in a very long time, Maya felt the pull of connection – gentle, unexpected, unmistakable – somewhere high above the world, between continents, between two strangers who didn't yet know how significant this moment would become.

By the time the flight attendant dimmed the cabin lights, Elias had dozed off, head tilted slightly toward her side. Maya glanced at him, watching the calm rise and fall of his chest. There was a peacefulness about him that she hadn't felt in months.

She turned toward the window, the first blush of dawn spilling across the horizon. Between sky and sea, the world blurred into watercolor hues – blue melting into rose, gold melting into dream.

Somewhere between Mumbai and Lisbon, she realized she wasn't just crossing time zones – she was stepping into a story she hadn't planned to tell.

And as if the universe wanted to seal the moment, the captain's voice cut through the quiet:
"Ladies and gentlemen, we'll be landing in Lisbon shortly. Local time is 6:05 a.m."

Maya smiled faintly, not knowing that this city – and the man beside her – were about to change everything she believed about love.

Chapter 2.

The Stranger by the Shore

Lisbon greeted Maya with a chill she hadn't packed for. The early morning fog hugged the narrow cobblestone streets, and the air smelled faintly of coffee, salt, and rain-soaked stone. The city was still half-asleep – except for the sound of tram wheels creaking along the rails, like an old song repeating through time.

She pulled her jacket tighter and followed the GPS on her phone toward the coast. The first shoot of her documentary was scheduled at Praia da Adraga, a quiet seaside village an hour from the city. Locals had told her it was a place where "the sea remembers."

Perfect, she thought. A poetic start for a film about love.

By noon, the sun had broken through the clouds, glinting across turquoise waves. The camera crew set up on the sand while Maya walked barefoot along the waterline, scouting frames. Every ripple, every glint of sunlight, every whisper of tide seemed to carry a story.

And then, there he was.

At first, she almost didn't recognize him – hair tousled by sea wind, sleeves rolled, trousers damp to the knee, crouching by a tide pool with quiet focus. A net and small underwater camera lay beside him.

Elias.

For a moment, Maya just stood there, watching him – that same calmness in his posture, that same gentle energy she'd felt on the flight. He hadn't noticed her yet.

"Hey, excuse me," she finally called, half-amused. "Are you following me across continents?"

He turned – and broke into a smile that made the horizon seem suddenly brighter.

"Maya," he said, almost laughing. "I could ask you the same. Didn't expect to see you in my backyard."

"Your backyard?" she teased. "So you live on the beach?"

"Pretty much," he replied, gesturing toward a small marine research cabin perched above the rocks. "I work here – collecting coral samples and documenting water conditions. It's not Bollywood glamour, but the ocean pays in peace."

She laughed softly. "So you're serious about this whole ocean lover thing."

He nodded. "Always have been. The sea is... constant. It doesn't change its heart easily."

Something about the way he said it made her chest tighten – a quiet sincerity she wasn't used to.

They fell into an easy rhythm as the afternoon stretched on, the ocean breathing calmly beside them. It was as if the world had softened its edges the moment they stepped onto the pier together — time unhurried, footsteps syncing without effort.

Elias slipped effortlessly into guide mode, showing her the shallow-water research stations along the coast. His voice warmed whenever he mentioned a species he loved or a reef he'd seen recover against all odds. There was a quiet conviction in him, the kind that made even scientific facts sound like stories worth holding on to.

Maya followed with her camera, filming as he knelt beside a tide pool.

"These little ones," he said, pointing to a cluster of anemones, "are stronger than they look. They rebuild even after waves tear them apart."

His tone was gentle, almost reverent.

Behind the lens, Maya captured the curve of his smile, the way his lashes flickered in the sun, the soft concentration in his brow. She zoomed in, framing the moment with an instinct that wasn't entirely professional.

"Can you talk about coral bleaching?" she asked, steadying her camera.

He stood, brushing the salt from his hands.

"When the water gets too warm, corals expel the algae that feed them. It's like..." He paused, searching for the right metaphor. "Like losing your voice. You're alive, but you can't speak. You turn pale. Silent."

Maya lowered the camera for a second, struck not just by the explanation, but by the sadness behind it.

"That sounds devastating."

"It is." He glanced at her. "But we try to bring them back. Little by little."

He walked ahead, sunlight throwing gold into the waves. She hit RECORD again.

She filmed him explaining restoration techniques, his gestures confident but unshowy. At one point, he crouched near a crate of equipment, and the sea breeze caught his hair, tossing it back with careless grace.

Maya swallowed.

Behind the camera, she found herself forgetting to breathe.

Elias turned to her unexpectedly.

"Is this okay?" he asked, a touch of shyness softening his voice. "I don't usually talk this much."

She blinked, realizing she'd been staring longer than intended.

"No, it's perfect," she said quickly. "You're perfect. I mean – your explanation. The footage. It's perfect."

A small smile tugged at his lips, amused and aware.

He moved closer, pointing at the screen.

"Do I really look that serious?" he asked.

"You look..."

She hesitated, adjusting the focus though it didn't need adjusting.

"You look like someone who cares. Deeply."

The compliment settled between them like warm sunlight.

He didn't look away.

For a moment, the only sounds were the soft slosh of waves against stone and the rustle of wind threading through the harbor ropes.

Elias stepped back only when a group of fishermen called out to him.

He waved, then turned to Maya with a sheepish shrug.

"Local celebrities," he joked.

She laughed, lowering her camera finally – as if releasing a breath, she'd been holding for hours.

Together they walked toward the research hut, every step wrapped in the comfort of a connection growing faster than either of them meant it to.

And behind her lens, Maya knew she wasn't just capturing footage anymore.

She was capturing him.

Unfiltered.

Unscripted.

Unaware of the way he was already becoming the heart of her film.

Later, as the crew packed up, a sudden drizzle began. The sky dimmed, waves growing restless.

"Come on," Elias said, grabbing her hand instinctively. "The café near the pier – it's safer there."

They ran across the sand, half-laughing, half-shivering, until they tumbled into a small seaside café. It smelled of cinnamon and roasted coffee beans. The windows fogged from the warmth inside.

Maya sank into a wooden chair, shaking off droplets from her hair. Elias handed her a steaming cup.

"For you. Best coffee in Lisbon – though I might be biased."

She took a sip – strong, rich, with a hint of chocolate. "You're not wrong," she admitted. "You could make a career out of this if marine biology doesn't work out."

He leaned back, studying her for a second. "So... are you still collecting love stories?"

"Yes," she said. "Real ones. Ones that last beyond convenience."

Elias's eyes softened. "Then you should talk to the ocean. It's loved this shore for centuries."

She smiled faintly. "Do you ever stop talking like a poet?"

"Only when someone stops listening."

That silenced her – in the sweetest way. Outside, the rain softened into a mist, and the café window framed them like a photograph: two strangers, half-soaked, half-smiling, in a city that didn't know what it had just begun.

When they finally parted that evening, Maya told herself it was coincidence – meeting him again. But as she walked away, her heart betrayed her logic.

Some stories don't need to be written.
They find you – again, and again – until you surrender to them.

Chapter 3.

Coffee, Cameras, and Chemistry

The next morning, Lisbon woke to the hum of trams and the smell of fresh bread from the pastelarias lining the streets. Maya had barely slept. Her mind replayed yesterday – the storm, the laughter, the warmth of a hand that wasn't supposed to matter.

She'd told herself it was nothing. Coincidence. Yet here she was, walking back toward the same café by the shore, camera bag slung across her shoulder, hoping – though she wouldn't admit it – to see him again.

And there he was.

Sitting by the window, sketching something in a small notebook, his coffee untouched. The early sunlight caught his profile – sharp jawline, soft eyes, that quiet concentration that made everything else blur.

He looked up, saw her, and smiled – the kind of smile that doesn't just reach the eyes, it pauses time.

"Maya Kapoor," he greeted, standing. "You're either following me or fate's working overtime."

"Let's give fate some credit," she said, trying not to smile too wide. "It's doing better than my GPS."

He laughed, motioning her to sit. "Coffee?"

"Always."

They ended up spending the entire day together.

Maya decided to feature Elias's coral restoration work in her documentary – not just for its environmental angle, but because of how alive he became when he talked about it. He took her on his small research boat, the Maré Alta, named after the tides. The sea stretched endlessly around them, a canvas of blue and silver.

As he adjusted the underwater camera, Maya filmed him. "You look different when you talk about the ocean," she said from behind the lens.
"How so?"
"Like you belong to it."
He smiled softly. "Maybe I do."

Back on shore, they shared sandwiches on a sun-warmed rock, watching the waves crash and retreat. She asked him about home, about family. He spoke of his mother, a painter who'd taught him patience through art, and of losing his father young.

When he asked about her, she hesitated.
"My parents are in Delhi," she said quietly. "My dad's a retired journalist – he still edits everything I send him. My mom... passed away when I was fifteen."
"I'm sorry," he said, voice gentle.
"It's okay," she replied, eyes on the horizon. "I think that's why I started making films. To hold on to moments before they disappear."

He looked at her for a long time – not with pity, but understanding. "Then maybe that's why we both ended up here," he said. "Trying to save what can't always be saved."

For a few seconds, silence stretched between them – the kind that says more than words ever could. The wind picked up, carrying the scent of sea salt and eucalyptus. Their hands brushed when they both reached for the same napkin. Neither moved away.

That evening, back in the city, they wandered through Alfama, the old district – all winding alleys and tiled walls, where Fado music spilled from open doorways. Lanterns glowed amber against the dusky blue sky.

"Lisbon feels like it remembers everything," Maya said softly.
Elias nodded. "That's why I love it. It keeps its scars beautifully."

They stopped near a street performer singing a mournful Fado tune – about distance, and longing, and the kind of love that survives silence. The crowd swayed gently. Maya's camera hung forgotten at her side.

Elias turned to her, voice low. "You know what's funny?"
"What?"
"I've met hundreds of people through my work. But somehow, I remember more from these last two days than from all of them combined."

Her heart skipped – once, sharply. She looked up at him, the lamplight catching the faint stubble on his jaw. "You talk like that often?" she teased, trying to hide her

nerves.
"Only when I mean it," he said simply.

For a moment, the world stilled – just the song, the night air, and the quiet gravity pulling them closer.

But before either could speak again, her phone buzzed – Riya, her producer, reminding her about the next day's shoot. Reality slipped back in, heavy and unwelcome.

"I should go," Maya said, stepping back slightly. Elias nodded, though his eyes lingered. "Of course. Tomorrow?"
She hesitated – then smiled. "Tomorrow."

As she walked away, the singer's voice floated behind her, soft and aching:
"Love does not ask for distance, only the courage to wait."

Maya didn't look back.

But she knew – deep down – she'd just met the one person who could rewrite everything she thought she knew about love.

Chapter 4.

The Night Lisbon Glowed

Lisbon shimmered that evening – as if the city itself had decided to dress up for them.

Golden light spilled over the terracotta rooftops, and the scent of grilled sardines and sweet custard tarts floated through the warm air. The streets of Bairro Alto buzzed softly with music, laughter, and clinking glasses.

Maya's camera hung from her neck, but she wasn't filming tonight.
Tonight, she wanted to feel – not capture.

She'd wrapped up the last day of shooting earlier that afternoon. Tomorrow, she'd fly to Madrid for the next part of her project. It was supposed to be just another stop on the itinerary, another story to tell.

But Lisbon had given her a story she didn't plan for – one that had a name, a face, and a smile that lived somewhere between calm seas and chaos.

Elias met her at Miradouro de Santa Luzia, one of the city's high lookouts.

The sun was setting, the sky painted in strokes of coral and violet. He wore a white shirt, slightly creased, and carried a paper bag.

"What's that?" Maya asked, curious.
He grinned. "Dinner. Sort of."

He led her to the ledge overlooking the city, and inside the bag were small boxes – local pastries, olives, cheese, and two tiny bottles of wine.

"This is your definition of dinner?" she teased.
"It's a Lisbon dinner. Small bites, big views."

They sat side by side, the city lights beginning to flicker below them like stars waking early.

They talked about everything – music, languages, their childhood dreams. Maya told him how she used to record monsoon rains as a kid, just to hear them later. Elias confessed he couldn't fall asleep unless he heard the sound of waves.

The night grew softer.

She caught him watching her once – not the way men often did, but as if memorizing something he didn't want to forget.

When she laughed at one of his stories, he said quietly, "I like that sound."

"What sound?"

"Your laugh. It feels like... sunlight."
Her heart tripped. "You really have no off switch for poetic lines, do you?"

"Maybe not," he said, smiling. "But I mean them."

As the air cooled, they wandered down the hill, the city glowing gold around them. Street musicians played violins under lampposts, couples danced barefoot in narrow lanes, and the scent of jasmine trailed through the night.

Maya felt something inside her shift – that quiet ache of wanting to stay in a moment longer than time allows.

By the riverside, the Tagus glittered under moonlight. Elias stopped walking and turned toward her.

"Do you ever think," he asked softly, "that maybe some people meet because they're meant to remind us what love could feel like – even if it's not forever?"

She looked up at him. "Do you think that's us?"

He didn't answer – not with words. The silence between them was thick, humming. His hand brushed hers, then lingered.
Maya felt her breath catch – the distance between them narrowing, the world fading to just the sound of the river and the city's hum.

For a second, he leaned closer – and she didn't move away.

But then, reality – the kind that creeps in just when dreams feel too vivid – broke through.
Her phone buzzed. Riya again. A reminder: Flight tomorrow at 8 a.m.

Maya blinked, stepping back slightly. "I should... get back. I have to pack."
Elias nodded, though disappointment flickered in his eyes. "Of course."

They walked in silence to the street corner where their paths would part.

He reached into his pocket and handed her something – a small, smooth seashell.

"It's from Praia da Adraga," he said. "When you miss the sound of this city, hold it close. It carries the ocean." She ran her thumb over the shell's surface – still faintly warm from his palm. "Thank you," she whispered.

They stood there for a moment – the night quiet around them, neither wanting to move.

Then Maya said softly, "Goodbye, Elias."
He smiled – that slow, soul-deep smile she'd never forget. "Até logo, Maya. Not goodbye. Just see you later."

When she returned to her apartment, she placed the seashell beside her camera.

As she packed her bags, she caught her reflection in the mirror – tired eyes, but softer.

Somewhere between the shots and sunsets, Lisbon had stopped being just another location. It had become a feeling.

And the man by the river – he had become a memory she wasn't ready to film over.

As she turned off the lights, the shell gleamed faintly under the moonlight – a small, silent promise of something unfinished.

Chapter 5.

The Countdown to Goodbye

Morning came far too soon.
Lisbon was still asleep under a pale silver dawn, and the world outside Maya's window was wrapped in that fragile stillness just before the city wakes.

Her suitcase sat open on the bed, half-packed. A tangled mess of camera cables, folded maps, and souvenirs – little pieces of a life she was about to leave behind.

She picked up the seashell Elias had given her. It felt impossibly light in her hand, yet heavy with everything she couldn't say.

Riya's voice echoed from the hallway. "Maya, the cab's here in twenty minutes! You sure you've got all your gear?"

Maya nodded automatically. "Yeah. Almost done." Her voice was steady. Her heart was not.

She glanced at her phone – no new messages. They hadn't spoken since last night. The silence between them felt deliberate, protective. Like both were afraid of saying too much, too soon.

She told herself it was better this way.
That she'd met him by chance, worked with him by luck,

and now life was moving forward – as it always did.
But her reflection in the window told another story – one of hesitation, one of quiet hope.

By mid-morning, she was at the pier where the team had first filmed Elias's marine lab. The sun shimmered across the water, and the salty wind tugged at her scarf.

He was already there, waiting.

He looked exactly the same and yet entirely different – hair tousled, sleeves rolled, a faint sadness shadowing his easy smile.

"I thought you'd left," he said softly.
"My flight's at eight tonight. I wanted to see the ocean one last time."

He nodded, eyes drifting toward the waves. "Goodbye visits are overrated," he said after a moment. "They make everything harder."

"Then let's not call it goodbye," she replied. "Let's just... walk."

They strolled along the shoreline, the sand cool beneath their feet, the breeze carrying the distant sound of seagulls and church bells.

Maya wanted to memorize everything – the rhythm of the waves, the warmth of his voice, the way sunlight caught in his hair.

They talked about trivial things at first – her flight, his upcoming research trip to Madeira, favorite songs. Both pretending it was just another conversation, not the last one they'd share for a while.

But beneath the small talk ran a steady undercurrent – don't forget me.

At one point, Maya stopped walking. "Elias," she said quietly. "Do you ever think some people are meant to meet at the wrong time?"

He looked at her – really looked – as if trying to read the thought behind her words.

"Maybe," he said. "Or maybe time's never wrong. Maybe it just tests us to see if love's worth waiting for."

Her throat tightened. "And if it isn't?" He smiled, but it didn't reach his eyes. "Then we'll know it was real enough to miss."

They reached the rocks where the tide foamed white against the shore. Maya crouched, running her hand through the cold water.

"I hate endings," she murmured.

Elias knelt beside her, close enough that she could feel his warmth even through the breeze.

"Then don't think of it as an ending," he said. "Think of it as a pause."

She looked up – his eyes soft, steady. For a moment, neither moved.

If the world had stopped spinning just then, she wouldn't have noticed.

But before the moment could turn into something irreversible, a distant horn broke the silence – the sound of a departing ferry.

Reality again. Always reality.

That evening at the airport, she stood by the gate, staring out at the runway lights. Her phone buzzed. A message from Elias. Just one line.

"Keep filming the world, Maya – but don't forget to live in it too."

She smiled through the ache. Typed back:

"And don't forget to listen to the ocean for both of us."

She hit send, then tucked the phone away.

As the plane lifted off, Lisbon shrank beneath her – a scatter of lights, a stretch of sea, and a city that had quietly stolen a piece of her heart.

She took out the seashell, held it against her ear. The faintest echo of waves whispered inside – and for the first time in years, she let herself cry.

Not from sadness. From knowing she'd found something real.

Some loves don't end when you say goodbye. They begin when you do.

Chapter 6.

Love in Time Zones

Two weeks.

That's how long Maya lasted before she broke her own rule – don't text him first.

It was midnight in Mumbai. She was editing footage, surrounded by a mess of coffee cups and scribbled notes. On her screen, the cursor blinked over an empty message window. Her fingers hovered – hesitant, almost embarrassed by how much she missed someone she'd only known for a few weeks.

Finally, she typed:

Hey, ocean man. How's Lisbon treating you?

She hit send before she could change her mind. And then, because fate enjoys playing favorites, his reply came within minutes.

Still loud with seagulls and coffee drinkers. The ocean misses your camera clicks. How's Mumbai?

She smiled, leaning back in her chair.
And just like that – the silence broke.

Emails became daily.

Texts became conversations that stretched through time zones.

Calls became confessions whispered into different nights.

When it was morning for Maya, Elias was wrapping up his day by the shore.

Their schedules had slowly grown into a routine – not one they planned, but one that felt as natural as breathing.

Maya woke to the soft buzz of her phone, sunlight spilling through the curtains of her Mumbai apartment.

And without even thinking, her first instinct was to check if he had sent something.

He always had.

A photo of the beach at dusk.

A short voice note about a fish that kept following their boat like a loyal dog.

A blurry selfie with his hair wind-tossed, apologizing for "looking like a shipwrecked scientist."

Maya would laugh into her pillow, heart tightening in that strange, sweet way distance teaches you.

Across the world, Elias would be ending his day by the Lisbon shoreline, shoes dangling from one hand, waves washing over his tired feet.

He sent her updates the way other people breathed: constantly, unconsciously, like she had become part of the rhythm of his days.

When it was midnight for her, it was evening for him – that soft Lisbon light she now knew by heart.

Maya stopped needing clocks.

She knew Lisbon evenings by the color of his voice.

Sometimes he called just as she sat on her balcony, the city outside quieting into night. The moment she answered, she could hear the ocean behind him – the wind brushing past the microphone, the gulls calling overhead, the low hum of a city settling into dusk.

"It's that golden hour again," she'd whisper.

He would flip the camera, showing her the sky – the way it melted from honey to rose, the faint silhouettes of fishing boats drifting near the harbor.

"This light really suits you," she'd tease.

"I'll tell the sun you approve," he'd reply, that crooked smile tugging at his lips.

Their worlds had become intertwined by rituals – little threads that crossed time zones with surprising strength.

Maya drinking chai while he sipped black coffee.

Elias sitting by the water while she lay curled under her blankets.

Her yawning mid-conversation while he tried not to laugh, whispering, "Go to sleep, Maya," in that gentle tone that made her chest ache.

The distance felt less like miles, more like a fragile thread of time – stretched, but never breaking.

Sometimes, they fell quiet on the call.

Not awkward silence – but the kind that felt like holding hands across galaxies.

She would listen to him breathe.

He would listen to her typing, editing, living.

Once, after a long pause, Elias murmured,

"Do you ever feel like we're on opposite ends of the same thread?"

Maya leaned back against her pillow.

"What do you mean?"

"I mean..." He hesitated, running a hand through his hair.

"The more we talk, the more it feels like time is the only distance left. Not place. Not oceans."

Maya's throat tightened.

And in a small voice, late at night and too honest to hide, she whispered,

"I feel that too."

The confession held them both still.

For the first time, the idea of wanting more – of needing more – was no longer something Maya could brush away as imagination or loneliness.

It was real.

Soft, fragile, growing.

A thread pulled gently between two hearts.

But even threads – even the strongest ones – begin to tremble when stretched too far.

And in the quiet hours before dawn, Maya sometimes lay awake and wondered how long a connection like this could survive on mismatched sunsets and borrowed time.

Yet every time she doubted, her phone lit up with his name.

A message.

A photo.

A silly joke.

A reminder of the shore that always returned to kiss the land.

And she held the thread again.

Gently.

Hopefully.

Like something worth fighting for.

One evening, Maya stood on her balcony, city lights glowing beneath her. The air was heavy with monsoon humidity.
Her phone buzzed – a video call.

Elias appeared, framed by the deep blue of twilight. Behind him, the Atlantic shimmered.

"Maya Kapoor," he said, smiling. "Still working, I see."
She laughed, brushing hair from her face. "Still flirting, I see."

They talked for hours – about everything and nothing. He showed her a dolphin that had been following his boat for days.
She showed him her messy editing room and joked about naming her coffee mug after him.

Somewhere between laughter and sighs, he said softly, "I wish I could be there to see you complain about deadlines in person."

Her heart fluttered – a small, dangerous sound. "Me too," she whispered.

Days turned into months.

Their lives unfolded in parallel – hers in crowded trains and editing studios, his among coral reefs and saltwater breezes.

Yet they shared sunsets through screens, meals over calls, and songs through playlists titled ours.

He sent her handwritten letters – real ones – pressed with dried sea lavender, describing the ocean like it was alive. She sent him small clips from her shoots – children chasing pigeons in Delhi, rain over rooftops, laughter spilling through chaos.

It was strange, how love could bloom without touch. How connection could feel more real through a grainy call than in crowded rooms.

But love across continents isn't just poetry. It's time – missed calls, lost signals, blurry connections.

One night, she called him, only for his voicemail to answer.

"Elias, hey," she said softly. "Just wanted to tell you – the film's premiering next month. I wish you could be here."

When he finally called back, it was 3 a.m. her time. "I'm sorry," he said, breathless. "The boat's engine failed mid-sea. We had no signal for two days."

Her heart unclenched. "You scared me." "I know," he whispered. "But if it helps – I missed you even when the ocean was louder than my thoughts."

She smiled, half-asleep. "That's cheating. You can't say things like that when I'm tired."
"Then sleep," he said. "I'll stay on the line until you do."

And he did.

She fell asleep to the sound of waves on his end – the soft lullaby of a love learning to breathe through distance.

As the calendar flipped to a new month, Maya realized something had quietly changed.

He wasn't just Elias, the man from Lisbon. He was home, in every way that word could mean.

But homes across oceans require faith.

And the tide, no matter how faithful, always tests what it touches.

Chapter 7.

Letters from the Sea

It arrived on a Tuesday – wrapped in brown paper, edges softened by travel, the faint scent of salt lingering on it. Maya found it in her mailbox, wedged between bills and flyers. Her name – Maya Kapoor – written in looping, careful handwriting she didn't need to guess.

Her heart stuttered.

Elias Rocha had sent her a letter.

No one wrote letters anymore.

But there it was – tangible proof that someone, somewhere, had thought of her long enough to let ink dry on paper.

Inside was a single folded sheet, the paper uneven and stained in places – as if it had sat on a damp desk overlooking the sea.

She unfolded it carefully.

Maya,

I was watching the tide pull away this morning – it reminded me of you.

How you leave a place but somehow, a part of you stays behind.

The ocean is quieter these days. Or maybe it's just me missing your noise – the way you fill silence with laughter, with questions, with stories about cities I've never been to.

I'm sending you a piece of the sea. It's pressed between the pages – sea lavender, my favorite. It survives salt and storms. I think you'd like that.

– E.

She read it three times. Then, she just sat there – smiling through tears she didn't expect.

Love, she realized, didn't always arrive in grand gestures. Sometimes, it came folded, inked, and smelling faintly of saltwater.

More letters followed.

Sometimes they arrived in neat envelopes, other times in slightly crumpled ones as if the journey had been rough, as if the wind and the salt air had argued with the paper on its way to her. Maya would run her finger under the flap carefully, almost reverently, the way one might open a gift that was not bought, but lived.

Each letter carried a fragment of Elias's world.

One arrived with a tiny white shell pressed flat between two pieces of tape, brittle but unbroken. Another had a few grains of sand sealed in a transparent packet – "from the tide that almost stole my notebook," he said. One envelope included a pencil sketch of dolphins leaping through the water, drawn during a quiet hour on deck. Another had cliffs so sharply shaded that they looked carved, not drawn.

Every time the postman came, her heart behaved the same way – a sudden leap, a breath held, a flutter in her chest like something small and bright had been released inside her.

She kept the letters in a wooden box – the one Noah had carved for her documentary scripts. Now it held a different story, one that felt like it was being written directly into her life rather than on film reels.

Elias's words always carried a rhythm, like the sea's tide brushing against the shore.

One evening, curled under a blanket and the warm spill of lamplight, she unfolded a letter that smelled faintly of salt.

You once said every story has a sound.

I've been thinking about that. The ocean sounds like your name sometimes.

Soft, then strong, then soft again.

Maya pressed the page to her chest for a long moment, letting the words settle into her bones.

Some letters were longer, full of details about his day – the equipment checks, the strange crustacean the crew found, the meals he loved or hated. Others were short, almost shy, as if he'd written them in a stolen moment between tides.

In one, he wrote:

I've started teaching the new interns.

They ask why I smile at my phone so often.

I tell them I'm talking to someone who believes in documenting hearts, not just places.

She reread that line more than any other. Not because of the compliment, but because it felt like he understood her work – understood her – in a way few ever had.

His most recent letter was written in blue ink, the strokes quick and slightly wind-blown.

The sea is colder this month.

The mornings bite a little. The nights bite a little more.

But the thought of you keeps it warm, in the strange way warmth works when distance should make things feel colder.

Maya read it slowly, allowing herself to feel the ache he embedded between the lines – not longing, exactly, but something deeper. Something that grew quietly, the way trust does. The way hope does.

And as she tucked the letter into the wooden box with the others, she realized something else:

Elias wasn't just sharing pieces of his world with her.

He was slowly stitching hers into his.

Maya wrote back, though her handwriting was messier – hurried between shoots, on airport napkins, or in the quiet of sleepless nights.

She told him about her film's progress, about how his letters became her favorite scenes to replay in her head. About how she sometimes replayed his voice messages just to fall asleep.

You're ruining me for normal life, Elias, she wrote once. Now even the rain feels like it's waiting for your name.

Then came the letter that changed everything.

It was longer than the others – and heavier.
Inside, along with his words, was a small silver pendant in the shape of a wave.

Maya,

You once asked me if I believe in fate. I said no. I believed in timing.

But you've made me rethink that. Because no timing could explain us – two people on opposite sides of the world, meeting because a flight got delayed and a filmmaker got curious.

I don't know where this will go. I only know I want to find out.
If you'll let me, I'll come to Mumbai after the expedition ends.

Yours,
Elias.

She read the last line until her eyes blurred. A thousand thoughts raced – fear, excitement, disbelief, hope. Could she handle seeing him again? Could their fragile, beautiful connection survive reality?

But before she could answer any of those questions, she smiled through tears and whispered to the letter, "Yes, Elias. Come home."

That night, she placed all his letters in a box – one she labeled The Sea Between Us.

And for the first time since leaving Lisbon, she fell asleep not missing him, but waiting for him.

Chapter 8.

The Visit

The morning air in Mumbai was thick with monsoon mist when Maya got the message.

Landing in two hours.

– E.

Just three words, but her pulse quickened like thunder. She'd rehearsed this moment for months – the arrival, the first hug, the words she might say.

But now that it was happening, she could barely breathe.

At the airport

She stood by the arrivals gate, clutching her phone, scanning every face. The world around her blurred into a moving crowd of families, greetings, and teary-eyed reunions.

Then – she saw him.

Taller than she remembered, skin sun-kissed, eyes searching the crowd until they found hers.

Time didn't just slow. It stopped.

He smiled first – that same crooked grin that once broke through her screen. And suddenly she was running.

He dropped his bag, met her halfway, and for a second, the world was just them.

No calls. No screens. No miles.
Only warmth, the familiar scent of salt and travel, and the heartbeat she'd memorized through imagination.

"You're real," she whispered against his chest. "So are you," he murmured, resting his forehead against hers. "Finally."

Their first days

Elias stayed in a small guesthouse near Bandra, a weathered two-storey building with peeling blue shutters and a balcony that opened toward the Arabian Sea. From his window he could see fishing boats bobbing like tiny, stubborn silhouettes, and at night the tide whispered against the rocks as if reminding him he was far from home but not alone.

Maya spent every free moment with him – slipping out between edits, meetings, and shoots to show him her Mumbai. Not the polished, postcard version tourists chased, but the one held together by spice and sweat and stubborn dreams.

She led him through narrow lanes where old markets breathed history. Vendors called out prices in a rhythm that felt like part of the city's heartbeat. Fabric shops spilled colors onto the sidewalks; the smell of roasting peanuts mingled with incense drifting from tiny temple corners.

Elias watched it all with quiet fascination, his steps slowing each time something new caught his eye – which was almost everything.

"Do you always walk this fast?" he teased as she tugged him into a lane packed with fruit sellers.

"If I slow down, Mumbai will walk over me," she said, grinning.

They paused for street-side chai, served in small glass tumblers that warmed their palms. He blew on the steaming surface carefully, then took a sip.

"It tastes like cinnamon and fire and... something else."

"Cardamom," she said, laughing. "And possibly dust."

He pretended to choke dramatically. She nudged him with her shoulder, and he nudged back, and for a moment the world shrank to just them and the clatter of cups.

As the sun dipped lower, they walked toward the sea. The city's lights flickered awake one by one – impatient, restless, glittering like stars that didn't want to wait for the sky. Cars rushed by in a constant ribbon of movement, honking in a strangely comforting language.

At Marine Drive, the wind tugged playfully at Maya's hair. They sat on the promenade, the concrete still warm from the day's heat. Below them, the waves crashed with the authority of something ancient, something that had shaped the city long before either of them existed.

Elias watched the water for a while, his face half-lit by the glow of passing headlights. Then, without showiness or hesitation, he reached for her hand.

His fingers were cold from the breeze; hers were warm from the walk. They met somewhere in the middle – not quite an admission, not quite a promise, but something unmistakably alive.

Maya didn't look at him immediately. She let the moment settle, let the sea breathe around them, let the city roar and hush and roar again.

When she finally turned, he was already looking at her.

"This place..." he said softly, "It feels like it keeps moving even when you stand still."

"That's Mumbai," she replied. "It'll exhaust you and fill you and break you and rebuild you – sometimes all before lunch."

He smiled, thumb brushing lightly over her knuckles as though memorizing them.

"And you?" he asked. "What do you do to me?"

She didn't answer. The waves answered for her, exploding against the rocks in a burst of sound, spraying cold mist at their feet.

But she didn't pull her hand away.

And he didn't let go.

"This place feels alive," he said.

"It is," she smiled. "It never sleeps, never apologizes." "Just like you," he teased.

She rolled her eyes – but blushed anyway.

But after the magic of reunion came something quieter, heavier – the truth of togetherness.

He was messy with his things.
She was impatient with plans.
He liked silence; she filled it with words.

They weren't video calls anymore. They were people – flawed, beautiful, stubborn.

One evening, while cooking together, Maya burned the curry and snapped,

"You could've said something instead of standing there!"
He looked startled. "I didn't know what to say. I didn't want to upset you."

"You already did," she said, then sighed, softening. "I'm sorry. I just... forgot how to be with someone in person again."

He stepped closer, resting his hands on her shoulders. "We're learning, Maya. This is easy to dream, hard to live. But I'm not going anywhere."

And just like that, the tension dissolved. They ended up eating burnt curry, laughing until it didn't matter.

<u>The night before goodbye</u>

Two weeks passed faster than either wanted. The night before his flight, they sat on the balcony of her apartment, the city lights flickering below.

"You'll go back tomorrow," she said softly. He nodded. "The expedition leaves in three days." "Will you come back?"

He didn't answer immediately. Then, quietly – "I want to. But I don't know when."

The words hung between them – heavy, honest, unfixable.

She rested her head on his shoulder. "Then let's not waste tonight."
They stayed like that – watching the city, feeling the clock tick, memorizing the silence they'd soon return to.

When he finally kissed her, it wasn't like their first – it was slower, deeper, like a promise whispered between goodbyes.

At the airport the next day, neither cried. He smiled, cupping her face. "The sea brought me to you once. It will again."

She nodded, even though her chest ached. "Go make it jealous, Elias."

He laughed softly, kissed her forehead, and walked away – back toward another horizon.

As she watched him disappear through the crowd, she thought of all his letters, the ocean between them, and how love – real love – was never about distance.

It was about staying, even when you had to leave.

Chapter 9.

The Drift

The apartment still smelled faintly of him—salt, coffee, and the citrus cologne he forgot on her shelf.

For a week after Elias left, Maya moved through her days like someone walking underwater. Everything sounded muted.

Even the city, with all its horns and chatter, seemed to pause and listen for a voice that wasn't coming.

She kept replaying the last morning: his wave through the glass, her forced smile, the blur of airport security between them.

She told herself it wasn't an ending—just another pause. But deep down, she could already feel the drift.

At first, they tried to keep the rhythm.
Daily texts.
Weekend calls.
Photos from both sides of the ocean.

But life doesn't wait for lovers.

Maya's film began streaming globally—interviews, press, new opportunities.

Elias's expedition sailed farther west, deep into waters without signal.
Weeks passed with missed calls and half-written messages.

Sorry, love. Connection's been rough. I'll call once we dock.
– E.

I miss you. But I'm proud of you.
– M.

She meant it. But pride didn't fill the silence at night.

One evening, she finally caught him online.
His face pixelated, sunburnt, tired.
"Hey, ocean man," she said softly.
He smiled. "Hey, filmmaker of chaos. How's fame?"
"Exhausting. How's the sea?"
"Endless."

They laughed, but it didn't sound like before.
There was distance not in miles, but in moments missed.

The call froze mid-sentence.
She waited five minutes before the screen went black.

It was 2 a.m.
She whispered to the silence, "Goodnight, Elias," knowing he wouldn't hear it.

A month later, they finally spoke again.
It started with joy. It ended with fear.

"You didn't tell me you extended the expedition," she said.
"I was going to. Things moved fast."

"You always say that."

"Because it's true, Maya. This is my work."

"And what am I?"

He exhaled. "Don't do that."

"I'm trying," she said, voice trembling. "But I can't be the only one trying."

Silence filled the call. The ocean roared faintly on his end.

Then he said, quietly, "Maybe we just need time."

She closed her eyes. "Time is the only thing we don't have."

The call ended without goodbye.

Days became weeks. No letters. No emails. The postbox that once felt magical now looked like a reminder of everything gone still.

Maya buried herself in work—shoots, meetings, deadlines. She smiled for cameras, but every time she heard the sea in her footage, her throat tightened.

One evening, she opened the box labeled The Sea Between Us.

Inside were his letters, tied with twine.

She untied them, let the words spill around her like pieces of a life she wasn't ready to lose.

If you'll let me, I'll come to Mumbai after the expedition ends.

She traced the sentence with her fingers and whispered, "You already did."

The monsoon returns

Outside, the first rains began – hesitant at first, like shy fingers tapping against the windowpane, and then all at once, a wild silver curtain pouring over the city. The monsoon had a way of transforming Mumbai into a living watercolor, blurring edges, softening chaos, making the familiar feel suddenly mythical.

Maya stood by the window, her forehead resting lightly against the cool glass. The city below shimmered – headlights turned into streaks of gold, streets into rivers reflecting broken neon signs, umbrellas blooming like dark flowers in every direction. The rain washed the world clean, but inside her, memories poured heavier than the storm.

She closed her eyes.

She could hear him again – Elias, laughing as waves crashed behind him, voice warm and soft when he spoke of the ocean.

"The sea sounds like your name sometimes."

He had said it so casually, as if it were simply a fact of nature, the way tides followed the moon.

Back then, the words had made her heart stumble. She didn't know what to do with something so beautiful, so unguarded. Now, she held onto them like a fragile shell washed ashore, the last thing the tide returned to her.

Lightning flashed, whitening the entire sky for a breathless second. Thunder followed, rolling through the clouds with a deep, aching growl.

For the first time, she whispered his name back to the storm.

"Elias..."

The sound left her like an exhale she didn't realize she'd been holding for weeks. It disappeared instantly into the rain-soaked air, swallowed by thunder, carried somewhere she would never see.

She didn't say it to call him home.

She didn't dare.

Home was oceans away, tangled in coral reefs, in Lisbon sunsets, in the salt that lived permanently on his skin. And she knew – painfully, quietly – that some distances weren't measured in miles but in choices, in grief, in the stories people weren't brave enough to finish.

She whispered his name to remind herself of something simpler.

That he had been real.

That their days had existed – the shared chai, the wandering lanes, the laughter on sunlit beaches, the soft brush of his fingers against hers at Marine Drive. That she hadn't imagined him into being the way she sometimes did with characters in her films.

She whispered it again, barely a breath.

"Elias..."

Not longing.

Not regret.

Just remembrance.

The rain ran down the window like tears she refused to shed. Somewhere above the roaring city, thunder answered her – softer this time, almost gentle, as if acknowledging her grief without demanding anything in return.

And for a moment, wrapped in the sound of the storm, she let herself feel everything she had been trying to outrun.

He was gone.

But the memory of him – warm, bright, impossibly tender – stayed.

Rainfall became the only witness to her quiet confession.

Chapter 10.

The Tide Returns

The monsoon had grown fiercer.
For three days straight, the sky over Mumbai was a sheet of silver rain.
Maya worked through it, pretending not to wait for something that might never come.

Until one evening – her phone buzzed with a message that made her drop her pen.

Maya,
I'm in Goa.
I couldn't go home without seeing you.
– Elias.

She reread it twice, afraid it would disappear like a dream.
Her heart, dormant for months, jolted awake.

She called him instantly.
The sound of rain merged with his voice – rough, tired, but still his.
"I thought you–"
"Didn't write?" he finished gently. "I know. I couldn't. Things got... complicated. But I'm here now."

"Why Goa?"
"Because it's closer to you than Lisbon."

And for the first time in months, she laughed through tears.

The decision

She booked a train the next morning.
Six hours through wet fields, foggy stations, and a heart pounding too loud to ignore.
Every drop on the window felt like the rhythm of his name.

When she finally reached, the air smelled of wet sand and nostalgia.
He was waiting near the shore, standing where the waves lapped at his feet.

The sight of him – hair windblown, eyes searching – undid months of distance in a single heartbeat.

"Hi," she said, breathless.
"Hi," he said, smiling softly. "You came."
"You asked."

And just like that, they were close enough to touch – again.

The confession

They walked along the beach, wordless for a while.
When he finally spoke, his voice was low, uncertain.
"I didn't mean to vanish. The expedition hit a storm off Madagascar. We lost a crewmate. After that... I didn't know what to say to you."
Her chest tightened. "Elias–"

"I didn't want to bring you into that darkness. You were my light, Maya. I couldn't ruin that."

She stopped walking.

It wasn't dramatic – no sudden gasp, no sweeping gesture – just a quiet, deliberate halt in the middle of the dimly lit street. The rain-soaked pavement reflected the faint glow of streetlamps, turning their puddled reflections into trembling halos of gold. The world around them had blurred into monsoon haze, but her voice cut through it like a clean, sharp line.

She turned to face him slowly.

"You don't get to decide what I can handle," she said, every word measured, soft but unwavering. "Love isn't about protecting someone from your storms. It's letting them stand beside you in the rain."

Elias froze.

For seconds, he said nothing. The rain dripped from his hair, traced soft paths down his jaw, soaked through his shirt until it clung to him like second skin. But he didn't try to brush it away. He felt it – every drop – as if the sky itself was echoing the turmoil inside him.

His throat bobbed.

"Maya..." he whispered, her name breaking in his voice like a wave hitting rocks. He looked at her the way someone looks at something they've lost before they even had a chance to hold it properly.

She waited.

Not impatiently.

Not pleading.

Just there – open, steady, braver than he felt.

Elias took one step toward her.

Then another.

By the time he reached her, his breath was trembling, his eyes glistening not just from the rain.

"I thought I was doing the right thing," he said, voice cracking at the edges. "Keeping the chaos of my life away from you. The ocean... the travel... the uncertainty... I didn't want you to drown in the parts of me that never stay still."

She swallowed hard. "You think I'm asking for safety? I'm asking for truth."

His jaw clenched – not in anger, but fear. The kind that came from loving someone so much it terrified you.

A long silence unfolded between them. Cars rushed by in the distance; a lone cycle bell chimed; thunder rolled far above. But here, in this small pocket of the storm, only the two of them existed.

Finally, he opened his mouth.

The words he had been holding, guarding, fearing.

"Then stand with me now."

The sentence escaped him like a confession, raw and unpolished. His voice shook – not out of weakness, but because something inside him was finally breaking open. His hand lifted slightly, as though reaching for her but afraid to assume she'd take it.

"Stand with me in this," he whispered.

"In the uncertainty. In the distance. In the mess that is my life. I don't know how to promise you the shore, Maya... but I can promise you the tide. I always return. If you'll let me."

Her breath hitched.

Rain pattered around them like applause from a sky that had been waiting for this moment.

Slowly, she stepped closer–one heartbeat, then another–until the storm blurred around them and his trembling exhale brushed her cheek.

She didn't touch him.

Not yet.

But her presence alone was an answer, as steady as the ocean he came from.

The reunion

He reached for her hand.

It was warm – familiar – like time had folded just for them.

The sky began to clear, streaks of orange spilling across the horizon.

The ocean that once separated them now shimmered before their feet, silent witness to their second beginning.

He pulled something from his pocket – a small, weathered envelope.

"I kept this letter," he said. "The one I never sent."

He handed it to her.
Inside, in his steady handwriting, were the words that ended the drift.

If I ever make it back, I don't want to start over. I just want to continue – from the moment you said yes.

Tears blurred her vision.
"Then yes," she whispered again. "Always yes."

He smiled – the kind of smile that made the world smaller and the heart larger.
The kind of smile that said home.

That night

They sat together on the sand, close enough for their shoulders to touch, far enough that the moment didn't feel rushed. The beach was almost empty–just a few distant figures and the rhythmic hush of the waves rolling onto shore. The night air smelled of salt and wet earth, the scent of a world washed clean after the storm.

The moon rose slowly, a pale silver lantern lifting itself from the horizon. Its reflection stretched across the water in a long shimmering path, as if inviting them to walk toward something gentle and new. It was quiet in a way the city rarely allowed—soft, sacred, unhurried.

For a long time, neither of them spoke.

There were no promises hovering in the air, no grand declarations waiting to be made. Just presence. The peace of two people finally breathing the same night, not separated by oceans, fear, or silence.

Elias let a handful of sand fall through his fingers, grains catching faint moonlight as they slipped away.

"Feels strange," he murmured, eyes fixed on the horizon, "being here with you. After everything... after the distance. It feels like I'm dreaming and the tide might wash it away."

Maya turned to look at him, her expression soft. "You're here now," she said. "That's enough."

A small gust of wind lifted a stray lock of hair across her cheek. Without thinking, without the hesitancy that once held him back, Elias reached out and brushed it aside. His fingers lingered for a moment—barely touching, yet saying everything.

His eyes searched hers, not with urgency, but with a quiet kind of wonder. As though he were memorizing her in moonlight, frame by frame.

"Do you still believe every story has a sound?" he asked, voice low.

She looked toward the waves as they curled and broke, steady as breath. "Yes," she whispered. "I always have."

He waited—because there was something about her pauses, her silences, that felt like part of the story too.

Maya smiled then, small but luminous, the kind of smile that didn't need the sun to exist. "And this one," she said softly, "sounds like waves coming home."

Elias inhaled sharply—not in shock, but in recognition. Like something he'd been carrying for years finally found its name.

The water continued its endless journey to the shore, each wave folding into the next, the sound both ancient and newborn. It felt like the sea itself had leaned in to listen.

He shifted slightly closer—not enough to blur the lines they'd carefully rebuilt, but enough that she felt the warmth of him against her side.

"Home," he repeated, tasting the word. "I never thought it could sound like this."

She glanced at him, eyes shining with unspoken things. "Maybe it was never a place for you," she said. "Maybe it was a person."

Their breaths mingled with the night breeze.

No kissing.

No declarations.

Just two souls learning the quiet language of belonging.

And for the first time, Elias understood what it meant for something–someone–to feel like the tide returning home after a long, restless journey.

That was the night the tide returned –
not to erase the distance, but to remind them that love, like the sea, always finds its way back.

Chapter 11.

The Return to Alfama

A year later.

The sea was quiet that morning in Lisbon – a soft whispering tide, the kind that carried memories instead of waves.
Elias stood on the pier, waiting for a familiar silhouette to step off the ferry.

The city behind him shimmered golden under the rising sun, the same place where it all began.

Then he saw her.

Maya – hair shorter now, a camera slung across her shoulder, eyes still filled with light.

She waved, and in that moment, time folded. The months apart, the long calls, the silence, the storm – all of it dissolved into the space between their smiles.

"You came back," Elias said, unable to stop smiling, the disbelief still softening the edges of his voice.

Maya stood in front of him, wind-tossed and glowing under the pale Lisbon sun. "You once told me the sea brings people back together," she said, tucking a strand of hair behind her ear. "I guess you were right."

He laughed–really laughed–something she hadn't seen in him for months. The sound echoed lightly against the old stone walls around them.

They began to walk through Alfama's winding lanes, the city unfolding around them like an old memory waking up.

The cobbled streets were the same ones they'd wandered years ago–when their hearts were reckless and untidy, when every street corner felt like a possibility, when they didn't yet know how deeply they would belong to each other.

Now, those same paths felt different.

Not new.

Not old.

Just right.

Laundry fluttered above them from wrought-iron balconies. Terracotta rooftops glowed warm against the morning light. The scent of fresh bread drifted from tiny pastelarias tucked between houses barely wide enough for two people to walk side by side.

Maya brushed her fingers along a chipped wall. "This place… it feels smaller," she said.

Elias nodded. "Maybe we just grew."

They shared a smile–the kind that didn't need translation.

As they climbed the familiar slope toward the overlook, the distant sound of Fado music threaded through the narrow streets. They passed the same tiled doorway where Maya had once joked that Lisbon felt like a city painted by someone in love.

It still did.

Now, it felt like a story finding its ending—not rushed, not forced, just... arriving.

Elias led her to the café overlooking the Tagus River, the place where time had once slowed for them, where stories were exchanged over steaming mugs and quiet glances.

The bell above the door chimed softly as they entered.

The smell hit her first—coffee, rain-soaked stone, and something warm and sweet she couldn't name.

"The same old man," she whispered.

Near the window, the elderly guitarist sat in his usual spot, hunched slightly with age but still coaxing music from the strings like someone in conversation with his memories. His fingers moved gently, weaving notes that drifted across the room like smoke.

He looked up briefly, eyes crinkling in recognition.

Maya felt a rush of warmth. The world had changed, years had shifted, hearts had broken and healed—but this café remained unchanged, a small sanctuary stubbornly untouched by time.

Elias pulled out her chair, just as he had the first time, and she sat by the window overlooking the river where sailboats glided like quiet thoughts across the blue.

"Does it feel strange being back?" he asked softly.

She looked at him—the man who had once been a beginning, then a heartbreak, and now something she didn't have a name for yet.

"It feels like the pages I didn't finish," she said. "And like I finally found the pen again."

The guitarist shifted into a new melody—slow, aching, beautiful.

Elias reached across the table, his fingertips brushing hers.

Not a request.

Not a claim.

Just a touch that said I remember you.

I've always remembered you.

Outside, the river glittered under the rising sun.

Inside, an unfinished love story inhaled deeply—

and began to turn its next page. But this time, they weren't strangers discovering possibility.

They were two people choosing permanence.

Chapter 12.

The Story She Chose

Over coffee, the world felt smaller–just the two of them, the soft clink of cups, and the gentle hum of the old guitarist's melody drifting through the café like a blessing.

Elias wrapped his hands around his mug, letting the warmth steady him. "Are you still traveling for your films?" he asked, though he already knew the answer. Maya was motion–she lived in motion. He had always loved that about her, even when it frightened him.

"Always," she replied, her smile soft but certain. "But this time, I pitched a series on oceanic conservation."

He looked up, brows lifting in surprise. She laughed at his expression.

"I thought I'd start... here."

He paused.

Not a long pause.

But long enough for his heart to stumble.

"Here?" he asked quietly.

"Lisbon," she said, voice steady but her eyes shimmering with the courage of someone taking a leap of faith. "Maybe for a year. Maybe longer."

Elias blinked slowly.

Her words sank into him like warmth spreading through cold water–slow, deep, undeniable. He searched her face, scanning every small expression, every flicker in her gaze, as if trying to confirm this wasn't something he'd imagined.

"Maya..." he said softly.

She didn't look away.

Her voice was casual, almost playful, but her eyes held the weight of everything they hadn't said for years.

Everything that had survived distance, storms, silence, and time.

He reached across the table, fingers brushing hers. Then he took her hand more firmly, like someone claiming something he had spent too long believing he didn't deserve.

"So," he murmured, his thumb stroking the back of her hand, "this is your next story?"

She inhaled, a small, shaky breath.

Then she shook her head gently.

"No," she said. "You are."

Elias's breath caught.

Not metaphorically.

Literally.

He forgot to breathe.

In that tiny café, with the scent of rain and roasted coffee and the guitarist playing a slow, aching tune, he felt something inside him shift—something that had been locked tight for too long.

"Maya..." His voice was barely audible. "You came all this way..."

"I didn't come for a place," she said, squeezing his hand. "I came for the person I couldn't forget."

He leaned back slightly, letting the truth of her words settle in his chest. It was overwhelming, beautiful, terrifying—all at once. His eyes glistened, softening, the way they had the first night he told her the ocean reminded him of her.

Outside, the Tagus shimmered as a gust of wind slipped past the windows like a sigh of relief from the universe itself.

"You're sure?" he whispered.

She smiled—not wide, not dramatic—just full of certainty.

"For the first time... completely."

Elias brought her hand to his lips, pressing a kiss to her knuckles.

Slow.

Reverent.

Like someone kissing the first line of a story he hoped would never end.

"This time," he said, voice trembling, "I'll stay for the whole story."

Maya's eyes softened. "Good. Because I'm finally ready to write it."

And in that quiet café in Alfama, with the river glittering behind them and the sound of Fado lacing through the air, two people who had once lost each other finally found the place their story was meant to begin again.

Chapter 13.

Where the River Meets the Sea

Later, they walked down to the shoreline, the sky blushing with the last remnants of sunset. The place where the Tagus River met the Atlantic Ocean felt almost sacred – a quiet merging of two vast worlds, a boundary and a beginning all at once. The water shimmered under the early night sky, the meridian line stretching faintly on the horizon like a silver thread stitching past to present, distance to belonging.

They stood side by side, the cool wind brushing against their skin. Maya closed her eyes for a moment, letting the scent of salt and evening air wash over her. It felt like both an ending and a beginning – the kind of moment that didn't need to be narrated to be understood.

"I used to think love was about crossing continents," she said softly, her voice blending with the breath of the waves.

Elias glanced at her, watching the way her hair moved in the wind, the way her shoulders carried equal parts strength and vulnerability. "It is," he replied. "But it's also about knowing where to stay once you've crossed them."

She turned toward him then, her eyes soft and luminous in the fading light. There was a steadiness in her gaze that hadn't been there before – a quiet certainty born not from impulse, but from choosing him over and over again, even in the distance, even in the silences.

"Then I'm staying," she whispered.

Elias's chest tightened with a rush of emotion–relief, joy, disbelief, everything he had been too afraid to hope for. A smile pulled at his lips, gentle at first, then wide and boyish, transforming him.

He wrapped an arm around her waist, pulling her close enough for the warmth of her body to chase away the chill of the ocean breeze.

"You sure?" he teased, voice low and warm. "I still leave socks everywhere."

She laughed–a sound he'd missed more than sunlight during stormy weeks at sea. "I know," she said, nudging him playfully. "And I still talk too much. Guess we're even."

"More than even," he murmured, brushing his forehead against hers.

They stood like that for a moment, a soft hush settling over them as the waves crashed nearby. The sound was steady, eternal, folding one tide into another, like time itself acknowledging their reunion.

Maya lifted her hand to his chest, feeling the slow, certain rhythm of his heartbeat beneath her palm. Elias cupped her cheek gently, his thumb tracing her skin as if memorizing the moment.

When he kissed her, it wasn't rushed.

It wasn't fragile or hesitant.

It was slow—anchored in all the miles they had crossed to reach this point.

A kiss shaped by longing and found again by choice.

A kiss like two shores finally touching after years of waiting for the tide to rise.

The ocean roared, wind curled around them, moonlight shimmered on the water – but they were the still point in the turning world.

Her fingers slid into his hair, and his hand tightened around her waist, deepening the kiss just slightly – enough to say I'm here without breaking the quiet magic of the moment.

When they finally pulled apart, their breaths mingling in the cool night air, Elias rested his forehead against hers.

"Welcome home," he whispered.

Maya smiled – soft, full, certain.

"I've been coming home to you for years," she said.

Together, they watched the meridian disappear into the darkening sea – not as a line that separated them anymore, but one that had led them right back to each other.

Epilogue

Where the Tide Rests

Months later, Lisbon had begun to reshape itself around them—not dramatically, not loudly, but in the soft, certain way cities embrace those who choose to stay.

Maya's series on oceanic conservation took life slowly, like the tide rolling in at dawn. Some mornings, Elias would walk her to the pier where she filmed the fishermen, their nets heavy with stories. Other days, she would wait for him outside the museum, listening for his footsteps in the rhythm of the city.

They didn't move quickly. They didn't need to.

One evening, they returned to the place where the river met the sea—their unofficial axis, their quiet meridian. The sun dipped low, turning the water molten, as if the horizon had melted just for them.

Maya tucked her hand into his coat pocket, a habit she'd picked up on colder nights.

"Do you ever think about how different things could've been?" she asked.

Elias nodded. "Sometimes. But then I remember... we still found our way back."

She smiled softly. "Across continents."

"And across time," he added.

A gull circled above them, its cry echoing into the widening dusk.

Maya rested her head on his shoulder. "I used to chase places. Always running, always filming the next thing. But now... I like the idea of being rooted."

"Rooted?" he teased gently. "In me?"

"In us," she said. "In this life we're building. Slowly. Carefully. Like sea glass."

He squeezed her hand. "Then let's keep building."

The sky darkened into indigo, the first star trembling into view.

She looked up at him with that familiar spark, the one he'd carried in memory for years. "Every story does have a sound," she whispered.

"And what does this one sound like now?" he asked.

She leaned in, lips brushing his.

"Like a home we didn't know we were searching for."

Elias kissed her—unhurried, certain—anchoring them to the moment, to the shore, to the life unfolding gently between them.

Behind them, the city lights shimmered.

In front of them, the ocean breathed.

And somewhere in the quiet, their story settled into the place it had always been heading:

Home.

THE END

About the Author

Swati Singh writes contemporary romance that explores the beautiful complexity of modern love across cultures, distances, and the barriers we build around our hearts.

Born and raised in India, Swati draws inspiration from her own experiences of connection and distance, in addition to her imagination of weaving stories that celebrate the courage it takes to love authentically in our globalized world.

When she's not writing, you can find her traveling to beautiful cities in and around the world, sipping coffee while watching sunsets, or collecting stories from strangers who become friends.

Love Across the Meridian is her debut novel.

Acknowledgements

Writing ***Love Across the Meridian*** has been a journey of heart, hope, and countless quiet moments of courage–and it would not have been possible without the people who stood beside me along the way.

To my family, whose unwavering love, encouragement, and faith in my dreams have been my greatest strength–thank you for believing in me even on the days I doubted myself.

To my husband and best friend, who listened to ideas, read early drafts, and reminded me to keep going–you have been my steady light through every chapter of this journey.

To the readers who will hold this book in their hands–thank you for giving my words a home in your hearts. Your trust and time mean more than you will ever know.

To everyone who inspired a line, a moment, a character, or a spark along the way–this book carries pieces of you within its pages.

And finally, to the version of myself who never stopped writing, even when it seemed impossible–thank you for choosing the story, every single time.

This book is for all of you.

With gratitude,
Swati Singh